FROGGY BUILDS A TREE HOUSE

FROGGY BUILDS A TREE HOUSE

by JONATHAN LONDON   illustrated by FRANK REMKIEWICZ

SCHOLASTIC INC.
New York Toronto London Auckland
Sydney Mexico City New Delhi Hong Kong

For Aaron, David E., Yasha, Sean, & Ely, and for Regina—who asked for it
   —J.L.
For Alex
   —F.R.

ISBN 978-0-545-46908-1

Text copyright © 2011 by Jonathan London.
Illustrations copyright © 2011 by Frank Remkiewicz.
All rights reserved. Published by Scholastic Inc., 557 Broadway, New York, NY 10012, by arrangement with
Viking, a division of Penguin Young Readers Group, a member of Penguin Group (USA) Inc.
SCHOLASTIC and associated logos are trademarks and/or registered trademarks of Scholastic Inc.

12 11 10 9 8 7 6 5 4 3 2 1   12 13 14 15 16 17/0

Printed in the U.S.A.   40

First Scholastic printing, September 2012

Set in Kabel

Froggy woke up
and looked out the window.
The sun was rising in the sky
like a giant pizza.

"Pizza!" sang Froggy.
And that gave Froggy a great idea!

He hopped out of bed
and got dressed—*zip! zoop! zup!
zut! zut! zut! zat!*

Then he flopped into the kitchen—
flop flop flop—and said, "Mom!
I'm going to build a tree house!
You can do lots of cool things
in a tree house without any
adults around! Like play cards,
tell jokes, and order out
for pizza!"

"That's nice, dear," said Mom.
"Are you going to build it all by yourself?"
"No, with a little help from my friends!"

Froggy hopped up and flopped
toward Max's—*flop flop flop.*

FRROOGGYY!

called his mom.

"Wha-a-a-t?"

"You forgot to eat your breakfast, dear!"

"I'm not hungry!"

When he got to Max's house, he yelled,
"Max! Max! Come out!"
And he told Max all about his great idea.
"Awesome!" cried Max.

And the two best friends
went over to Matthew's . . .

and Travis's . . .

and came back to Froggy's
house with hammers, nails,
saws, and boards.

Then they started building
the tree house
(with a little help from Dad).
First, they sawed boards—
zee-zaw! zee-zaw!

Then they nailed them to the trunk
so they could climb up—*zing! zang! zunk!*

Then they built a floor.

FWWOOGGYY!

called Pollywogilina.
"Wha-a-a-t?"
"Me wanna help!"

"GO AWAY!" cried Froggy.
"NO PESKY LITTLE SISTERS ALLOWED!"

Froggy started to saw a branch—
zee-zaw! zee-zaw!

FRROOGGYY!

called Frogilina,
hopping over the fence.
"Wha-a-a-t?"

"You're sawing yourself off
with the branch! Hee hee hee!"
"Oops! I know that!" cried Froggy.
"NOW GO AWAY!
NO GIRLS ALLOWED!
JUST ME AND MY FRIENDS!"

Froggy and his friends
started putting up boards for the walls.
"Oops!" cried Froggy—
but only a few boards fell.

Then he started pounding nails again—
zing! zang!—ZZOWW-WEEEEE!

"I'll kiss it!" cried Frogilina.
"Yuck!" cried Froggy. "GO AWAY!"

He climbed down
and held up his thumb to his mom.

Mom put a Band-Aid on Froggy's thumb.
"Now do you want something to eat?"
"Not until we finish our tree house,"
said Froggy.
"Then we'll call out for pizza!"

But by the time they finished the tree house—
the sun was setting!
Froggy dropped his hammer—*zonk!*—
"Oops! Watch out b-e-l-o-o-o-o-w!"
and yelled, "We're sta-a-a-a-r-r-r-viiing!
We want to call out for pizza NOW!"

Froggy's mom climbed up, called
Swamp Pizza, and let Froggy order:
"We want an EXTRA large pizza—
with lots and lots of flies!"
"Not on my slice!" said Max.
"Not on my slice!" said Matthew.
"Not on my slice!" said Travis.
"Whatever!" said Froggy.

When the pizza finally came . . .
Froggy grabbed the box
and started climbing up.

He climbed and the
pizza wobbled . . .

FROGGYS TREE HOUSE
BOYS ONLEY!!

"Oops!" cried Froggy,
looking more red in the face than green.

"Caught it!" cried Frogilina.
"Wow!" cried Froggy.
"Lucky catch!"

"I have a surprise for you, Froggy!"
said Frogilina. "If you let me into
your tree house."
"Well . . ." said Froggy.
"Only if I like the surprise!"

So Frogilina scampered up like a monkey,
opened the box, and said,
"Surprise!"
And sprinkled on lots and lots of flies!

"YES!" cried Froggy. "Yippee!"
And he took a big bite.
"Yum! This pizza's frogilicious!
Let's call out for another one!
Wait! Let's make that FIVE pizzas!"

And Froggy and his friends ate pizza—*munch crunch munch* . . .

played cards—*slap slap slap* . . .

and told jokes . . .

in Froggy's tree house . . .
all night long.